The LOST CAR

The LOST CAR

V. Gilbert Beers

Illustrated by Tonda Rae Nalle

VICTOR BOOKS

A DIVISION OF SCRIPTURE PRESS PUBLICATIONS INC.
USA CANADA ENGLAND

Copyright © 1994 by Educational Publishing Concepts, Inc., Wheaton, Illinois

Text © 1994 by V. Gilbert Beers

Published in Wheaton, Illinois by Victor Books/SP Publications, Inc, Wheaton, Illinois.

ISBN 1-56476-314-5

Printed in the United States of America
1 2 3 4 5 6 7 8 9 10 - 98 97 96 95 94

TO PARENTS AND TEACHERS

What does your child do when a problem comes along? How does she respond to it? Where does he find the solution?

What we need is a good role model—someone who faces problems as we do, but knows the right way to resolve them. The Muffin Family is a role-model family. They face problems much like the ones that bother us daily. But there's a difference. The Muffins are not quite like their neighbors. You will soon learn that they are Christians, and thus they meet their problems with Bible truth.

The Muffins aren't perfect. Neither are you and I. But they are Christian. They aren't free from problems. But they resolve them—God's Way.

If you're looking for a book that will role-model Bible truth at work in a family much like yours, meet The Muffin Family.

V. Gilbert Beers

Maxi Muffin wasn't very careful about his room. You might say it was a messy room. That's what Mini Muffin said whenever she went by the door.

"Inviting pigs to play here today?" Mini would say. But Maxi pretended not to hear her.

Poppi poked his head through the doorway.

"You certainly keep your room neat and clean," Poppi would say. Of course Poppi didn't mean that. Maxi knew that Poppi was teasing.

"For a moment I thought I lost my way," said Mommi. "I thought this was the city dump." Maxi was so busy playing that he barely heard that.

Maxi built a tower with his building set. He should have put the pieces away.

But he didn't.

He sailed paper airplanes around his room.

Now it looked like an airport.

15

He played marbles on the floor.

Of course you know
what happened when he
finished.

When BoBo came to play
with Maxi, he thought Maxi's
room was great.

That's because BoBo's room was just as messy.

Mini's friend Maria said something like "disgusting," but Maxi pretended that he didn't hear her.

"What does a girl know about a boy's room anyway," Maxi grumbled.

Later that day Maxi lost his favorite toy, a wonderful little car that could zoom across his room.

He looked here. He looked there.

He looked everywhere.

Maxi looked and looked and looked and looked. He wanted to cry. But he knew that wouldn't help find his car.

Then Mommi came into Maxi's room.

"Need some help?" she asked.

"Please," said Maxi.

Mommi began to put some of Maxi's toys neatly on the shelves where they belong. "We don't need to clean up my room," said Maxi. "We just need to find my car."

But Mommi kept on putting toys on the shelves and clothes in the closet where they belonged. Maxi began to help her. As Maxi was putting the last pile of toys on the shelves, he found his car. He was so happy. "Thank you, Mommi," he said.

At that very moment Grandmommi walked into Maxi's room. All of Maxi's toys were put neatly on his shelves, and clothes were hung in his closet.

"Maxi, what a neat room you have," said Grandmommi. "I'm so proud of you for keeping your room so clean. Some boys are like pigs. But you are such a neat, clean boy."

Maxi smiled a big smile and hugged Grandmommi with a big hug. He loved his Grandmommi very much. He would do almost anything to please her, even keep his room neat and clean.

Maxi's room wasn't ALWAYS neat after that, but it wasn't quite as messy either. Whenever Maxi's room got a little messy, he thought about what Grandmommi said. Then he picked up his toys and clothes.

And it didn't seem like hard work. It just felt good to make other people happy.